MY STRONG MIND

II

THE POWER OF POSITIVE THINKING
by NIELS VAN HOVE

Published in Australia by Truebridges Media

First published in Australia 2019

National Library of Australia Cataloguing-in-Publication entry
Creator: Van Hove, Niels
Title: My Strong Mind: The Power of Positive Thinking
ISBN: 978-0-6480859-4-2 (eBook)
ISBN: 978-0-6480859-5-9 (Paperback - KDP)
ISBN: 978-0-6480859-6-6 (Hardback - IngramSpark)
ISBN: 978-0-6485641-0-2 (Paperback - IngramSpark)
Target Audience: For primary school age
Subjects: Juvenile fiction. Confidence in children. Self-esteem. Toughness (personal trait).

Cover layout and illustrations by Diki (graphic designer)
Typesetting by Nelly Murariu (PixBeeDesign.com)
Printed by Kindle Direct Publishing & IngramSpark

Disclaimer
All care has been taken in the preparation of the information herein, but
no responsibility can be accepted by the publisher or author for any damages
resulting from the misinterpretation of this work. All contact details given in this book
were current at the time of publication, but are subject to change.

Dedicated to Daphne's
strong mind and positivity

Jack is a **kind** and **happy** boy.
He **likes** school and has many **hobbies**.

But like every boy, he sometimes
faces **difficult** situations at
home or at school.

- He gets **disappointed** with himself
- He finds it hard to make **new friends**
- He gets easily **upset** and **angry**
- He feels **pressured** by children to do things he doesn't like

At school, his friend Kate told him
that your mind is
very **strong** and **powerful.**

You can **train** your mind to decide
what to **think** about yourself,
about others, or about **any situation**.

You can tell your strong mind how to react to your **fears** and **worries**.

This helps you to stay **positive**, be yourself, and be at your best.

Jack decided to use his strong mind with all his **challenges**.

That evening, he **wrote down** some things he **did not like** about himself.

Playing soccer badly, **struggling** with piano lessons, a **poor** test result at school, having few friends. However, behind every **disappointment** he wrote something **positive** about himself.

He called this his **Positive List!**

Positive List

Jack's Positive List **helped** him to remember what
made him **proud**. He could always use it to
be **confident** and stay positive about himself.

The next day at school,
Jack wanted to make **new friends**, and
spotted a group of boys playing soccer.
At first, he didn't **dare** step forward.

Then he thought about his **Positive List** and all the things that made him proud. This gave him **confidence**, and he walked over to the group to say hello.

Later on, some boys **dared** Jack to throw
a stone through a school window.
They **teased** Jack and told him:
'You're a chicken if you don't do it.'

Jack **counted to 10** to calm himself down. He told the boys he could **make up** his own **mind** and didn't feel like doing these kinds of things. Then he walked off.

In the school vegetable garden,
Jack found a **bird** with a **broken** wing.
He **felt sad** for the bird and
softly started **crying**.

16

Some kids saw this and laughed at him. But Jack thought: *it's OK to have emotions. I'm just being sad.* He gently picked up the bird and looked after it.

17

When Jack arrived home, he couldn't find his favourite toy. He got **upset** and so **angry** that it felt like his head was about to **explode**.

His mother **calmly** walked him to the kitchen and asked, 'Jack, how **big** is your **problem**?'

19

On the fridge, Jack read a **Problem List** he had made together with his parents.

- **Ginormous**: you need a lot of help from an adult
- **Big**: you can solve it with some adult help
- **Little**: you can solve it with a little reminder
- **Tiny**: you can fix it all by yourself

20

'I think it might be little,'
Jack said, calmer now.

'Well, shall I **help** you
find your toy then?'
his mum asked.

Mum and Jack tried to
find his toy **together**.

That evening Jack was **learning** to play
a **new song** on his keyboard. But he kept
hitting the wrong notes all the time!

Jack was **frustrated** and felt like
giving up. Then he told his mind:
keep trying your best, you can do it!

He kept **trying** and
finished the song
without any mistakes.

Jack felt
very **proud.**

23

As Jack was getting **ready** for bed, he thought about the school camp he had the next day.

Jack was a little bit scared to go **camping** for two days, and was **nervous** about being **away** from home.

Whilst his dad was tucking him in, Jack asked, 'Daddy, is it **OK** to be a bit **different** sometimes and to be **afraid** to go **away** from home?'

'You're **fine** just as you are Jack,' said his dad. 'And of course it is **OK** to be scared sometimes. I've been **scared** many times in my life.'

His dad smiled. 'Everyone feels a little bit scared when doing something for the very first time. But that's how we learn.'

Jack felt comforted that it was OK to have fears.

Jack was tired from a long day.
He was less worried about
school camp and happily fell asleep.

And his mind grew
just a little bit
stronger that day.

NOTES FOR PARENTS

What is Mental Toughness?

Mental Toughness* is a combination of resilience, the curiosity and drive to grow yourself, and confidence in your own abilities and interactions with people. Mental Toughness has been used in elite sport psychology for many years to increase performance, and it applies to everyday life too.

There are four attributes that characterise Mental Toughness, also called The Four Cs:

Commitment: I set goals and work hard to deliver them.

Control: I'm pro-active and keep my emotions in check.

Challenge: I stretch myself and learn from everything.

Confidence: I have the ability and can stand my ground.

Research shows that mentally tough children perform up to 25% better in exams. They sleep better, are more engaged in the classroom, and have higher aspirations. They also transition more successfully from junior to secondary education, perceive less bullying, and are less likely to adopt anti-social behaviour.

Like us, we can be sure our children will have to deal with adversity, stress, and challenges during their life. Mental Toughness is a plastic personality trait and can be developed or improved. The examples in this book show how small interventions and positive thinking can lead to better outcomes.

---

* Refers to *Developing Mental Toughness: Improving Performance, Wellbeing and Positive Behaviours in Others* by Peter Clough and Doug Strycharczyk.

As an introduction for parents to Mental Toughness and many intervention techniques, I suggest my free e-book *Building Mental Toughness: Practical help to be yourself at your best*. This free book is available on my website **www.mentaltoughness.online**. Here you can also download fun exercises to do with your kids. Including – How big is my problem? – as described in the story.

ABOUT THE AUTHOR

Niels is a father of two girls and lives with his wife in Melbourne, Australia. He is a mental toughness coach and author who enjoys getting the best out of individuals. With his books, he hopes to make a positive difference, promote conversation, and help children learn about confidence, resilience and a positive mindset. Niels is the founding coach at **www.mentaltoughness.online**.

ABOUT THE ILLUSTRATOR

Vanlaldiki is a digital artist and an illustrator from Mizoram, India. As a child, she found interest in drawings after her dad drew his idea of a new home with colorful sketch pens. She is known for her love of digital arts as well as traditional ones. Additionally, she is fond of pets, kids, nature, and trekking. You can find her other works on **dykkyartz.weebly.com**.

www.mentaltoughness.online

Made in the USA
Columbia, SC
24 May 2020